oe pulled back a corner of the
blanket. Inside the bundle was
a tiny bird with a stripy orange
and white beak and bright-
orange webbed feet. It was an
adorable baby puffin!

Look out for:

Zoe's Rescue Zoo

The Picky Puffin

Amelia Cobb

Illustrated by **Sophy Williams**

nosy
crow

With special thanks to Natalie Doherty

For Fiona and David.
Congratulations on your wedding, and may all of your puffins be perky!

First published in the UK in 2017 by Nosy Crow Ltd
The Crow's Nest, 14 Baden Place, Crosby Row,
London, SE1 1YW, UK

Nosy Crow and associated logos are trademarks and/or
registered trademarks of Nosy Crow Ltd

Text copyright © Hothouse Fiction, 2017
Illustrations © Sophy Williams, 2017

The right of Hothouse Fiction and Sophy Williams to be identified as the author
and illustrator respectively of this work has been asserted by them in accordance
with the Copyright, Designs and Patents Act 1988.

A CIP catalogue record for this book will be available from the British Library

Printed and bound in the UK by Clays Ltd, St Ives Plc

Papers used by Nosy Crow are made from wood grown in sustainable forests.

ISBN: 978 085763 983 7

www.nosycrow.com

Chapter One
A Special Project

Zoe Parker smiled as the school bell rang.
It was Friday afternoon and the end of
lessons for the week. Zoe couldn't wait
for the weekend to start!

"I'd like to set you all some homework
to do over the weekend," explained Zoe's
teacher, Miss Hawkins, as Zoe and her
class packed away their pencils and

books. "I want you all to do a project on something you love. You can pick anything – a place you like visiting or even your favourite thing to eat. I want to read all about it, and find out why you love it so much."

Zoe's heart leapt. Miss Hawkins always set her class really fun projects – and Zoe already had an idea of what she could write about!

"What are you going to do your project on?" asked Zoe's friend Nicola as they walked out into the

playground together.

Zoe grinned. "An animal, of course!" she replied. "I just don't know *which* animal. It's so hard to choose."

Zoe thought she was the luckiest girl in the world, because she lived at a very special zoo! Her Great-Uncle Horace was a famous animal expert and had started the Rescue Zoo years ago to give homes to animals who could no longer live in the wild. Zoe's mum, Lucy, was the zoo vet. Zoe thought her home was the most special place to live. She spent all her spare time with the animals and helping the zoo keepers with their jobs. One day she wanted to be a zoo keeper herself.

What animal shall I do my project on? she thought as she walked home with her mum. *I love elephants, tigers and pandas...*

3

*And I really like wolves, peacocks and puffins
too. And then there are the hippos, the bats
and the gorgeous polar bears. And grey mouse
lemurs, of course!*

Zoe's best friend at the zoo was a tiny grey mouse lemur named Meep, who had big golden eyes, soft, silky fur and a long tail. He didn't live in an enclosure like all the other animals, but with Zoe and her mum in their little cottage at the edge of the zoo instead. He was small and cute, and could be *very* cheeky.

Zoe shook her head. There were too many animals to choose from! *Maybe I'll have a good idea when I get back to the Rescue Zoo*, she thought to herself.

As Zoe and her mum were finishing their plates of spaghetti that evening, the phone rang. Zoe jumped up and answered it. "Hello?"

"Zoe!" cried a familiar voice. "It's me – Great-Uncle Horace."

"Where are you?" asked Zoe eagerly. "Are you still travelling around Iceland?"

Although Great-Uncle Horace had started the zoo, he spent most of his time travelling around the world, helping out animals who were lost, poorly or in danger. He sent Zoe lots of postcards from his adventures, and sometimes he brought a new animal back to the zoo if it was in urgent need of help, to give it a safe and special home.

"Actually, Zoe, I'm on my way back to the Rescue Zoo right now – and I have an animal emergency. Can I have a quick word with your mum?" asked Great-Uncle Horace. He sounded very serious.

Zoe passed the phone to her mum and waited as Lucy spoke into the phone in a low, urgent tone. "We'll be there right away," she said, then hung up the phone and grabbed her coat. "Come on, Zoe. We'll have to do the washing up later."

Zoe quickly scooped up Meep, who'd been nibbling a banana on the chair next to hers. She pulled on her coat and followed her mum outside. "Where are we going?" she asked.

"To the river," Lucy replied. "Great-Uncle Horace is sailing back to the zoo in the Rescue Zoo boat and we're going to meet him there."

Zoe wanted to ask what the animal emergency was, but her mum was walking quickly ahead. She turned to Meep. "What do you think's happening?" she asked him. Zoe didn't just love animals. She had a very special secret: she could talk to them too! It made living at the Rescue Zoo even more amazing. No one else knew about her unusual gift though – not even her mum or Great-Uncle Horace.

Meep shook his head. "I don't know, Zoe," he chirped. "Maybe he's found a penguin with a sore flipper?"

"I think it sounds more serious than that, Meep," replied Zoe. "Come on!"

She caught up with her mum and raced alongside her, with Meep holding tightly to her shoulder. They ran past the giraffes, the lions and the pandas, and took a shortcut down to the river, which ran right past the zoo.

As they arrived, panting, Great-Uncle Horace's boat pulled into sight. The Rescue Zoo symbol – a bright red hot-air balloon – was painted on its sail.

Zoe's heart started beating fast as she saw Great-Uncle Horace up on the deck. Normally he looked so happy and jolly, but now he seemed very worried indeed. She wondered what animal he was bringing back to the zoo, and what was wrong. Would it be very badly hurt, or frightened? *I just hope we can help!* she thought, crossing her fingers for luck.

Great-Uncle Horace steered the boat towards the bank and threw out a rope to Lucy, who quickly tied it to a post on the bank so that it wouldn't float away. Then he stepped on to land. An elegant blue bird with a curved yellow beak sat on his shoulder. It was Kiki, Great-Uncle Horace's hyacinth macaw, who went everywhere with him. Great-Uncle Horace was holding a small wooden box, and inside the box was a shivering bundle wrapped in a blanket.

"What is it?" asked Zoe. On her shoulder, Meep leaned forward for a better look.

Great-Uncle Horace smiled at Zoe and pulled back a corner of the blanket. Inside the bundle was a small bird with a stripy orange and white beak and bright-orange webbed feet. It blinked up at Zoe nervously. The bird's feathers were covered in patches of something sticky and dark.

"Is it a baby puffin?" Zoe asked.

Great-Uncle Horace nodded. "She is indeed. Or rather, she's a puffling. That's

11

what baby puffins are called. She's only a couple of months old. I found her on my travels around Iceland. More than half the puffins in the world live there. But I'm afraid she got herself into a sticky situation, as you can see."

Zoe looked at the dark splotches on the puffling's body. "What's on her feathers?" she asked. "Is it mud?"

Great-Uncle Horace shook his head sadly. "I'm afraid it's oil, Zoe," he explained. "A big container of oil leaked into the ocean very close to where this puffling lived. It ruined the homes of many puffins. When I found this little one, she was all alone and in great danger. I tried to get as much of the oil from her feathers as I could but, as you can see, she needs another wash."

"Let's get her to the zoo hospital," said Lucy, taking the box. "Come on!"

They ran back through the zoo and past the meerkat enclosure, where a family of curious meerkats popped their heads up to look as they all rushed past.

When they got to the zoo hospital, Lucy quickly unlocked the door and led them all inside.

"We need to clean the oil off the puffling," Lucy explained. "Uncle Horace, please can you fetch some washing-up liquid from the cupboard?"

Great-Uncle Horace gently placed the puffling, still wrapped in its blanket, on the worktop and hurried into the store cupboard. The puffling's bright, stripy beak peeked out over the top of the blanket and it gave a sad little cheep.

Zoe stared after Great-Uncle Horace. "Washing-up liquid?" she said, puzzled.

Lucy, who was filling a basin with warm water at the sink, nodded. "It may sound strange, but washing-up liquid is a really good way to clean birds or other animals who have been affected by oil spills," she told Zoe. "You'll see."

The puffling let out another frightened squeak. Quickly, Zoe picked up the little bird and gave it a cuddle. As her mum and Great-Uncle Horace poured washing-up liquid into the basin and mixed up a soapy, bubbly mixture, she took it aside and whispered quietly in its ear, "Don't worry. You'll be safe here, I promise! I'm Zoe, and this is Meep."

"Hello!" squeaked Meep from Zoe's shoulder. "What's your name?"

The tiny puffling cheeped weakly.

"Piper! That's a lovely name," Zoe whispered.

"Zoe, we're ready to clean the puffling now," called Lucy.

Zoe carried Piper over to the basin full of warm soapy water.

"We're going to give her a bath!" Lucy explained. "Lower her in very carefully, Zoe."

Zoe did so, whispering encouragingly to the little puffin, who shivered nervously. Then Lucy showed Zoe how to gently rub the oil out of each feather, one by one.

"What would happen if we left the oil in her feathers?" asked Zoe.

Great-Uncle Horace looked sad. "She'd become very ill indeed," he said. "She might even die. You see, like lots of birds, puffins use their beaks to keep their feathers clean. It's called 'preening'. This baby has already tried to clean the oil from her feathers with her beak, and she's accidentally swallowed some of the oil. That's why she's so weak — it's given her a very poorly tummy."

"Poor little puffling," Zoe said gently, stroking another feather clean. "Having a poorly tummy is horrid."

"Puffins also use their feathers to keep themselves warm," Lucy added. "But if they get oil stuck in them they stop working properly and the puffins can become very cold. That's why Great-Uncle Horace had to rush back from his trip. It was so important to get all the oil out of the puffling's feathers quickly."

Zoe nodded. It was even more serious than she had thought. "So once she's nice and clean again, she's going to feel lots better?" she asked.

"That's right!" Lucy replied with a smile.

Zoe gazed down at the tiny bird, who was quietly cheeping. "She's very lucky you found her, Great-Uncle Horace. And we're lucky too – she's so sweet."

"She is very sweet," agreed Great-Uncle

Horace, smiling at the puffling. "I must admit, I've always had a soft spot for puffins."

"I love puffins too!" Zoe grinned. "In fact, they might be one of my favourite animals of all." Suddenly an idea popped into her head. "I know! I'm going to do my school project on her."

"School project?" asked Great-Uncle Horace, as Meep gave a puzzled squeak from Zoe's shoulder.

Quickly, Zoe explained that she had to write a project on something she loved. "I knew I wanted to write about an animal – but I couldn't decide which animal I liked best. Now I've decided – I'll write about the puffling!"

Meep jumped off Zoe's shoulder with a squeal and scampered over to the other side of the room. "What are you doing, Meep?" Zoe asked. But she was distracted by the puffling, who opened her little beak and managed a louder cheep.

"It sounds like she's feeling stronger already!" Great-Uncle Horace said, looking very pleased.

"Time to get her dried off," said Lucy, fetching a large fluffy towel from the store cupboard.

Zoe lifted the bird out of the water and passed her to Lucy, who gently rubbed her dry. Zoe stroked the puffling's snowy-white tummy. It looked so much better now the splotches of oil were gone.

"She looks so cute," Zoe said. "I love the black feathers on top of her head – it looks like she's wearing a cap."

Lucy laughed. "Yes, it does."

Zoe helped Lucy arrange some warm, thick blankets into a nest in a quiet corner of the hospital and put Piper in the middle.

"We'll let her get some rest and come back in the morning," said Lucy.

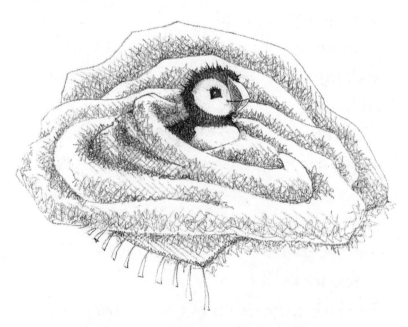

"Goodnight, Piper!" whispered Zoe as she left the hospital. "See you tomorrow!"

Later that night, as Zoe got into her stripy tiger pyjamas, she couldn't stop talking about the puffling. "Her beak is so beautiful, Meep. I love the stripes!" she said. "And did you see her orange feet? And her cute little black eyes. They looked just like shiny buttons. I think she might be the sweetest animal who's ever come to the Rescue Zoo!"

"I'm really glad Great Uncle Horace managed to rescue her," Meep said, wriggling under the bedcovers.

"Me too," said Zoe, snuggling in beside him.

"I won't ever get oil in my fur, will I, Zoe?" Meep asked.

"Oh, Meep, no of course not. Oil spills only happen in the middle of the ocean." She cuddled the little lemur tight. "You're not planning on moving out to sea, are you?"

"Definitely not!" Meep exclaimed. "I don't like getting wet!"

Zoe smiled and then switched off the lamp beside her bed. "Let's go to sleep." She was feeling really tired now – and the sooner tomorrow came, the sooner she could visit Piper!

Chapter Two
Piper the Puffling

"Goodness, Zoe! You're up early," said Lucy as she walked into the kitchen the next morning.

Zoe was sitting at the kitchen table with a big sheet of paper spread out in front of her and a pack of coloured pencils scattered around. "I woke up early and I was too excited to go back to sleep," she explained. "I wanted to start my school project straight away. Do you like it?"

Lucy came over to look. Zoe had drawn Piper the puffling in the middle of the sheet of paper. She had spent lots of time adding each feather on the puffling's body with her sharpest black pencil. Around the puffling were lots of brightly coloured hearts with facts about puffins written inside them. The biggest heart was right above the puffling's head, and Zoe had written PIPER inside it.

"Wow, Zoe, it looks fantastic!" Lucy said. "Is Piper the name you've chosen for the puffling?"

"Er, yes," said Zoe. "Do you like it?"

"It's lovely," said Lucy.

"When can we go and visit Piper, Mum?" Zoe asked. "I want to see how she is this morning."

"Let's have some breakfast first," Lucy said, going over to the kettle.

Meep scampered on to the table, holding half of a banana that he was chewing for his breakfast. There were bits of soggy banana around his mouth too – Meep was a very messy eater! "Zoe, you've been doing your project for ages and I'm bored. Let's play!" he squeaked, hopping up and down.

Zoe smiled at her little friend. "In a minute, Meep," she whispered, being careful not to let her mum hear. "I just need to finish colouring in the puffling's feathers."

She reached for a black colouring pencil but cheeky Meep jumped in her way, sticking his tongue out. Zoe couldn't help giggling. Meep loved to be the centre of attention. But as Meep scampered around the table, Zoe realised he was leaving banana paw-prints all over her project!

"Stop it, Meep!" she said, moving the sheet of paper away quickly. "Look at what you've done to my project." She grabbed a tissue from a box on the table, trying to clean the banana off the paper. "Oh, Meep. I've been working so hard on this all morning and now it looks really messy."

Meep slipped under the table as Zoe wiped the banana off her project. "I'd better leave it to dry," she said, placing it carefully near the radiator. "I'll do some more later on, when we come back from visiting Piper."

After breakfast, Lucy agreed that it was time to pay the little puffin a visit. "Let's hope her poor tummy's feeling much better today," she said. "At least we managed to get the last of the oil from her feathers so she should be nice and warm again."

As Zoe walked through the zoo with her mum and Meep, animals called out to her from either side of the path. Everyone at the Rescue Zoo always loved hearing about new arrivals, since almost every animal at the zoo had once been rescued by Great-Uncle Horace!

"Who did Great-Uncle Horace bring

to the zoo last night?" Oscar the African elephant trumpeted as they walked past his enclosure.

"Is it another hippo?" Hetty the hippo asked.

"Please let it be another hippo," Henry the hippo called from the pool at the centre of their enclosure. "I could teach it how to dive."

Zoe just smiled and shook her head. She couldn't answer them properly in

front of her mum or the trickle of early
morning visitors already at the zoo.
They'd think she was crazy! Then she
had a great idea. If she just talked loudly
about the puffling to her mum all the
way to the hospital, the other animals
would overhear and know what was
going on.

"So, Mum," she said loudly. "Isn't it exciting to have a NEW BABY PUFFIN at the zoo?"

"Yes, Zoe, it is," Lucy replied.

"It's a puffin," she heard Oscar trumpet.

"Ah, a puffin," Henry said, before splashing back underwater.

As they walked past the panda enclosure Chi Chi and Mei Mei came scampering over.

"Has someone new moved into the zoo?" Chi Chi asked.

"Is it a panda?" Mei Mei asked shyly.

"I just can't believe a A NEW BABY PUFFIN has come to stay," Zoe said to her mum loudly.

Lucy stared at her. "Yes, it is very exciting. But there's no need to shout about it."

Oh yes there is! Zoe thought to herself.

By the time the hospital came into view Zoe's voice was hoarse and her mum probably thought she was crazy but at least the other animals knew about the new addition to the zoo.

"Oh, the door's unlocked," Lucy said, pushing it open.

"Maybe Great-Uncle Horace got up early too," Zoe said. But as soon as they walked in, her heart sank. Standing by the puffling's bed, holding a clipboard and a pen, was the zoo manager, Mr Pinch. He was always dressed in a spotless zoo uniform, with not even a speck of dust to be seen. His polished shoes were shining and, as usual, he was frowning. Piper the puffling was huddled nervously in her nest of blankets. Her bright, stripy beak

the only part of her that
was visible.

"Mr Pinch!" Lucy
exclaimed. "We
don't usually see
you at the zoo
hospital. How can I
help you?"

"I'm here to make
a record of the new
animal," Mr Pinch
announced. "I need all
her details – type of
bird, age, weight and
date of arrival at the
zoo."

Lucy gave Mr Pinch
all the information,
and he wrote

everything down. "Mr Higgins told me the bird was covered in oil when she arrived," he said disapprovingly. "What a mess!"

"She's not a mess at all!" said Zoe, feeling cross. "We gave her a bath yesterday and cleaned all the oil from her feathers. And it wasn't her fault that the oil leaked from a container."

"Well, I'm glad to hear she's clean now," replied Mr Pinch grumpily. "I hope I don't have to spend all my time tidying up after her, like I seem to do with every other animal!"

As Mr Pinch marched out of the hospital Meep stuck his tongue out at his back.

"He's so annoying!" Zoe exclaimed.

"Never mind Mr Pinch," Lucy smiled.
"We've got a fun job this morning.
Feeding Piper! Will you check outside
the back door, Zoe? I asked Will, the
penguin keeper, to deliver a bucket of fish
for us. Puffins and penguins have fairly
similar diets."

Zoe ran to the back door of the zoo
hospital and found a small plastic bucket
with a pile of silver herring inside. She
carried it inside and set it down next to
Piper's nest of blankets. The little bird
looked curiously at the bucket.

"Do you want to try feeding her a fish,
Zoe?" asked Lucy. "Herrings are a special
favourite for puffins, and especially puffin
babies. Puffins don't chew their food, you
see – they swallow it whole. So they need

to eat very thin types of fish, like herring
and hake."

"So this is perfect for Piper," said Zoe.
She picked up a fish by its slippery tail
and held it out in front of Piper's beak.
The little puffin looked at it sadly, then let
out a tiny squeak.

"Oh dear. She doesn't seem very keen," said Lucy.

Zoe understood what the puffling had said. "Maybe the oil in her tummy is still making her feel sick?" she suggested.

Lucy nodded. "Yes, that could be it. Poor Piper! We'll put the fish in the fridge and try again later. I think part of the problem is that she's not feeling very at home in the hospital. She needs a proper puffin burrow. Will tells me there's a spare enclosure near the penguins, with plenty of water. We'll make a burrow there for her tomorrow, if she's strong enough."

"OK," said Zoe. "I hope she will be!"

As Lucy went to check on the other animals in the zoo hospital, Zoe reached out a hand and gently stroked the puffling's feathery black cap. Piper just sat there quietly.

"She's a bit of a picky puffling, isn't she?" Meep whispered from Zoe's shoulder. "She doesn't seem to want to do anything!"

"I'm sure it's just because she's not feeling well," Zoe whispered back.

"But she doesn't even like eating!" Meep replied. "Who doesn't like eating? Eating is the best thing in the whole world." He scratched his little head. "Or maybe playing is. I'm not sure. Let me see. . ."

The little lemur sprang off Zoe's shoulder and on to the ground, where he tried a cartwheel and then a wobbly somersault.

Zoe couldn't help giggling – until Meep lost his balance and, with a squeal, toppled head-first in the bucket of fish.

"Bleurgh! I'm all slimy and smelly!" he chattered crossly, scrambling out.

"Oh, Meep!" sighed Zoe. "Now we're going to have to clean you up. Stay there."

She quickly filled a bowl with warm water and told Meep to climb in.

"I hate water. I hate it nearly as much as stinky, smelly fish," Meep grumbled as he wriggled about, splashing water everywhere.

"Meep, stop wriggling!" Zoe said sternly. "You're making me all wet too."

Meep looked sad. "You didn't shout at Piper when she had to have a bath yesterday."

"Yes, but it wasn't Piper's fault that she had to have a bath. And Piper didn't make me soaking wet!" Zoe replied, frowning at her furry friend.

As soon as Zoe had lifted Meep out of his bath and towelled him dry, she went back over to Piper. "I hope you feel better really soon," she said. "You're going to love it here at the Rescue Zoo. All of the other animals are really friendly."

Piper tilted her head to one side and cheeped.

Zoe shook her head. "I'm afraid there aren't any other puffins here. But there are lots of penguins. And there are hippos and elephants and pandas and otters… Oh, just you wait and see. It's such a fun place to live."

Piper nodded but she still didn't look very happy. But then Zoe never felt happy whenever she had a poorly tummy. As soon as Piper was feeling better she'd be a lot brighter, Zoe was sure. She turned round to look for Meep but there was no sign of the little lemur. *He must have gone home to get warm after his bath,* Zoe thought. Oh dear, she couldn't wait for both Piper and Meep to be happy again!

Chapter Three
Burrow Building

The next morning, Zoe made Meep a special breakfast. "Chopped strawberries and peaches," she whispered to him as she put the bowl on the kitchen table.

"Yum!" Meep chirped and began tucking in. "What are we doing today, Zoe?" he asked, popping three pieces of strawberry in his mouth all at once.

"Today we're going to do something really exciting," Zoe said.

"Cool! Are we going exploring?" Meep asked, waving his little paws in excitement.

"Er, no…" Zoe replied.

"Are we going to jump out of trees on top of the chimpanzees?" Meep asked hopefully, popping a piece of peach in his mouth.

"No! We're going to help Piper build a burrow," Zoe explained. "Mum thinks she's strong enough to leave the hospital now."

Meep wrinkled his tiny nose and pulled a face. "That sounds like a bit of a boring job."

"Come on, Meep, that's not very nice," Zoe whispered. "Piper needs a burrow to live in. And I think building it is going to be lots of fun."

"OK," Meep sighed, throwing a piece of strawberry in the air and catching it in his mouth.

There was a loud knock on the front door.

"I'll get it," Lucy called from upstairs, where she was getting ready for work.

A few moments later Great-Uncle Horace came striding into the room. Kiki was perched on his shoulder and he was holding a couple of trowels.

"Good morning!" he boomed. "The sun is shining and the birds are chirping. It's the perfect day for burrow-building."

"Are you going to be helping us build a burrow, Great-Uncle Horace?" Zoe said excitedly.

"I certainly am," Great-Uncle Horace replied. "Your mum's needed back at the hospital."

"OK, I'll be off then," Lucy said, coming into the kitchen and picking up her coat. "Have fun burrow-building!"

Once Zoe and Meep had finished their breakfast they walked through the zoo with Great-Uncle Horace. Zoe felt so happy to be spending some more time with her great-uncle. Normally he had to rush straight off to rescue another animal in need. As they went past each enclosure the animals called out excitedly. They all loved Great-Uncle Horace as much as Zoe did. After all, if it wasn't for him they wouldn't be at the zoo!

"Good morning, monkeys!" Great-

Uncle Horace bellowed, as the monkeys swung from the branches of the trees, chattering excitedly.

"Good morning, Shadow!" Great-Uncle Horace called, as they passed the wolf enclosure. "My, how you've grown."

Zoe smiled as she remembered how Great-Uncle Horace had brought Shadow to the zoo at Halloween when he was just a little pup. Shadow was much bigger now, and his fur was sleek and shiny in the sun.

"Piper should be in her new enclosure by now," Great-Uncle Horace said as they approached the penguin enclosure. "I asked Will to go and fetch her from the hospital and start settling her into her new home."

As they walked past the penguin enclosure Pip came waddling over to the fence.

"Hello, Zoe," he squawked. "I hear

there's a new puffin at the zoo."

Zoe nodded and smiled.

"Goodness, is that Pip?" Great-Uncle Horace asked.

Pip flapped his wings excitedly.

"Yes," Zoe replied, grinning as she remembered how small Pip had been when he'd first arrived.

"Come and tell me all about the puffin soon," Pip squawked.

"I will," Zoe whispered, and she hurried on after Great-Uncle Horace.

"Here we are," Great-Uncle Horace said as they reached the enclosure behind the penguins. There was a stream running through it, with wide, muddy banks. Pretty willow trees lined the stream, their branches dipping down into the water.

"Oh, it's lovely," Zoe cried.

Meep leapt from her shoulder and scrambled into one of the trees, jumping from branch to branch. The little lemur clearly loved the puffling's new home as much as Zoe did. She hoped Piper would like it too. Zoe spotted Will by the

stream. Piper was next to him, pecking curiously at the mud with her bright, stripy beak.

"Good morning!" Great-Uncle Horace called to them. "Your burrow-builders have arrived."

"Hello!" Will smiled as they walked over.

"How is she?" Zoe asked, looking at Piper. The little puffling flapped her wings.

"Much better than yesterday," Will replied. "Could you look after her while I go and feed the penguins?"

"Of course!" Zoe crouched down on the bank next to Piper. "Hello," she said with a smile as she gently stroked the puffling's head. Piper flapped her wings even faster and this time she lifted off the ground.

"Look, she's flying!" Zoe exclaimed.

"So she is," Great-Uncle Horace replied with a chuckle.

Piper flew round and round in a circle, then landed back on the ground.

"She's like a little feathery helicopter," Zoe said with a giggle. She turned to see if Meep had seen but he was still busy jumping from tree to tree.

"Right, let's start digging," Great-Uncle Horace said, kneeling down on the bank and starting to dig a hole with his trowel. "Normally puffins would make their burrows in the rocks but as we don't have anywhere as rocky as Iceland here in the zoo we'll make one in the ground instead."

Zoe and Piper stood and watched as

Great-Uncle Horace started digging a burrow. "The burrows have to be just the right size," he explained. "The puffins need to feel cosy and safe."

"This is going to be your new home," Zoe whispered to Piper. "Do you like it?"

Piper tilted her head to one side, as if she wasn't sure.

"Once the burrow's finished we'll get some straw to line it with, to make it nice and warm," Great-Uncle Horace explained.

"Can I do some digging?" Zoe asked.

"Of course!" Great-Uncle Horace stepped back and let Zoe take over. "Be careful to dig nice and slowly though. If you dig too fast the hole might collapse and then we'll have to start all over again."

As she carefully dug, Zoe imagined Piper tucked up all snuggly in her new burrow and she couldn't stop smiling. She was definitely going to write about this in her school project!

"OK, Zoe, I think that's big enough,"

Great-Uncle Horace said after a while. "Let's see if she'll go in."

They both stood back and watched as Piper looked at the burrow. She waddled a bit closer, gave a sad little cheep, then turned and walked away.

"She doesn't like it," Zoe said, feeling really disappointed.

"I told you she was picky," Meep chirped from a nearby branch.

"Maybe it's too big," Zoe said to Great-Uncle Horace.

"Hmm, could be," he replied.

"I'm going to dig a smaller one." Zoe heard Meep give a sigh as he swung off to another tree.

In the end, Zoe dug several different burrows but every time the same thing happened. Piper would waddle over and inspect the burrow, then waddle off again without going inside. Zoe wished she was on her own with the little puffling, then she'd be able to talk to her and find out what was wrong.

"Can we go and do something else now?" Meep said, scampering over.

Zoe shook her head. She wasn't going to leave here until Piper had a burrow she liked. She couldn't bear the thought of the little puffling sleeping out in the cold.

"I'm going to go and get some straw," Great-Uncle Horace said. "Maybe that will do the trick."

As soon as Great-Uncle Horace had gone, Zoe turned to Piper. "What's wrong?" she asked, crouching down beside her. "Why don't you like any of the burrows?"

But before Piper could reply Zoe heard a loud cough behind her.

"And what, may I ask, is going on here?"

Zoe turned to see Mr Pinch standing there, staring at the four freshly dug piles of mud.

"Oh, we were just digging a burrow for the new puffling," Zoe explained.

"A burrow?" Mr Pinch snapped. "This doesn't look like a burrow – it looks like a whole street of burrows! I've never seen such a mess."

"We were just trying to make one the right size," Zoe said. "I'll tidy up, I promise."

"Hmm." Mr Pinch frowned and shook his head. "I'll be coming back to check this afternoon." And with that he turned and marched away.

"OK." Zoe's heart sank as she saw Piper's head droop. Why did Mr Pinch have to be so grumpy all the time? It was so annoying – especially when she was trying to make Piper feel welcome. Just then she saw Great-Uncle Horace making his way back with an armful of straw.

"This'll make your burrow so much cosier," she whispered to Piper. "Just wait and see."

Zoe helped Great-Uncle Horace line

each of the burrows with some straw.
Then they turned to look at Piper.

The puffling waddled closer and tilted
her head to one side.

"Aha!" Great-Uncle Horace cried. "I
think this might just have done the trick."

"I bet she still doesn't like them," Meep
called from a nearby tree.

Zoe ignored him and continued
watching Piper. The puffling waddled
even closer to one of the burrows and
took a good look inside.

"Go on, Piper," Zoe whispered.

But the little puffling wouldn't go any
further. With a nervous squeal, she took
a few steps back on her orange feet and
shook her head firmly. *Oh no!* thought
Zoe.

Up on his branch, Meep let out a groan.

"She's the pickiest puffin I've ever seen! I'm not picky. I like everything!" He leapt into another tree. "I like bananas and strawberries and peaches and playing and jumping and being brave."

Zoe frowned at Meep. She wished she could tell him to stop showing off.

"My word, Meep's certainly full of beans," Great-Uncle Horace chuckled.

Zoe was very relieved that he couldn't understand what Meep was saying.

"Look at me, look how brave I am!" shouted Meep, swinging into the branches of the tree closest to them. "Look at—Aaaahh!"

Meep was so busy calling down to Zoe that he'd stopped paying attention to what he was doing. His tiny fingers missed the branch and he tumbled to the ground! Zoe's heart thumped, but luckily the nimble lemur landed safely – right next to where Piper was standing.

With a frightened squeak, Piper darted away from Meep – right into the nearest burrow! She huddled inside the cosy hole, peering out anxiously.

"Meep!" Zoe scooped the little lemur up into her arms. "That was very naughty," she whispered in his ear so Great-Uncle

Horace wouldn't hear. "You could have really hurt yourself. And you really scared Piper!"

Meep stared at Zoe. "But I made her go into her burrow!" he chattered indignantly. "That's what you wanted, isn't it?"

Zoe sighed. "Yes, I did," she whispered. "But not like that!"

Chapter Four
Mischievous Meep

Later that evening, Zoe put the finishing touches to her school project and showed it to her mum.

"It sounds like you had lots of fun building the burrows," Lucy said as she read it.

"I did," Zoe replied.

"Tell her who made Piper go inside the

burrow," Meep said, jumping on to the table.

Zoe frowned and shook her head. She was still a little cross about how Meep had behaved earlier.

"Your teacher's going to be so impressed with your work, Zoe," said Lucy.

"I hope so!" said Zoe. "I just wish. . ."

"What?" asked Lucy.

"Well, now that Piper is feeling better I wish my class could meet her," Zoe explained. "They'd be so excited to meet a real-life baby puffling."

"Hmm, well, she did seem much better today. . ." Lucy said, looking thoughtful. "Maybe I could have a word with Miss Hawkins."

Zoe's heart leapt with excitement. "You mean – ask if we can have a class trip to the zoo?"

"I'll have a chat with her tomorrow," Lucy said. "I'm sure we can arrange something."

As Zoe jumped up to give her mum a hug, she heard Meep sigh. "All this fuss over a picky puffin," he chattered. "What if she still doesn't want to do anything? Your class will get so bored!"

"I hope they get here soon!" said Zoe, bouncing up and down excitedly.

It was three days later and Zoe was waiting impatiently at the zoo gates. Today was a school day – but Zoe had been allowed to come home at lunchtime as it was a special occasion. This afternoon Zoe's class was paying a visit to the Rescue Zoo! Lucy had spoken to Zoe's teacher, Miss Hawkins, and they'd arranged a special trip for them to visit Piper the puffling.

"Do you think they'll see my sign, Mum?"

Lucy smiled at the banner Zoe had made the night before. It was pinned to the zoo gates, and said in big, rainbow-coloured letters: MISS HAWKINS' CLASS – THIS WAY TO THE PUFFIN!

"I don't think they'll be able to miss it, Zoe," she replied.

Meep, who was perched on top of the gate, gave a snort. "I still don't understand why your class is coming all this way to see the pickiest puffin in the whole world," he muttered.

"Shh!" Zoe whispered, shaking her head at the little lemur. She hoped that Meep would be good when her class arrived.

From down the street, Zoe heard an excited shout. "Look, there's the zoo gate! And there's Zoe!"

Zoe grinned and waved as her class appeared, all chatting excitedly about their trip. "Hi, everyone," she called.

"Welcome to the Rescue Zoo," Lucy said with a smile.

"Thank you for having us," Miss Hawkins replied. "What a treat this is. You know, I've never seen a real puffin before, so I can't wait to meet my very first!"

"But have you even seen a mouse lemur before?" Meep yelped, running along the top of the fence.

"Oh, look at that tiny monkey!" cried Thea, one of Zoe's schoolfriends. "He's chattering away like he's talking."

"That's Meep. He's actually a grey

mouse lemur," explained Zoe. "Although lemurs are related to monkeys."

"I think he's even cuter than a monkey," added another of Zoe's friends, Jack.

"I've got to get a picture of him," Thea said, taking a camera from her school bag. "He's so sweet."

Meep's face brightened as one by one Zoe's classmates took pictures of him.

"Let's go and see Piper the puffin," Zoe said after a few minutes. She couldn't wait for her class to meet the zoo's new arrival. "Follow me."

When they got to Piper's enclosure the tiny puffling was huddled inside her burrow. She poked her black-capped head out as the crowd of children lined up by the fence.

"Here we are," said Zoe. "This is Piper's

new home and that's the burrow I built
for her with my Great-Uncle Horace."

Zoe's classmates gasped as they saw
the little bird. "Wow, Zoe. She's so teeny!"
cried Zoe's friend Louis.

"Yes, she's still very young," said Zoe.

"I love her stripy beak," Jack said.

"Me too," said Zoe.

"She looks sad," said Thea. "Is she OK?"

Zoe looked at the little puffling and realised that Thea was right. Piper did look sad. "She has been quite poorly but she's getting better," she explained. "Perhaps she's feeling hungry. Mum, can we try to give Piper some food?"

"Of course." Lucy unlocked the gate of the enclosure and walked inside. She fetched a small bucket of herring from a little store cupboard at the back. Piper had started eating again now, although she was still quite picky about which fish she ate.

Zoe crossed her fingers as Lucy held out a fish to the little puffling. Piper gave it a sniff, then turned away.

"Oh no!" cried Zoe's friend Nicola. "She doesn't like it."

"Maybe she'd prefer another kind of fish?" suggested Louis.

"Maybe she doesn't like fish at all. I don't like it very much, except fish fingers," said Jack.

"I told you," chattered Meep, who was sitting on a nearby branch. "She's picky!"

The cheeky lemur leapt from his branch
on to the top of the fence and scampered
nimbly along it, right in front of Zoe's
class. "Look at me instead!" he chirped,
sticking out his little tongue and waving
his paws. "I'm loads of fun."

Zoe's classmates started to giggle.

"He's so funny!" chuckled Jack.

"He really is," Miss Hawkins said.
"Perhaps if the puffin isn't feeling very
well, you could tell us a bit about this
little chap instead?"

Zoe frowned at Meep. The cheeky
little lemur was taking all the limelight
from Piper – on purpose! But she knew
she couldn't talk to Meep now, with
all her class and her teacher listening.
"Of course," she replied. "Well, Meep's
special because grey mouse lemurs are

only found on the island of Madagascar. They're one of the smallest primates in the whole world – the size of a mouse, which is where the name 'grey mouse lemur' comes from. He loves all types of fruit, and he also eats seeds, flowers and nectar."

As Zoe talked about Meep the little lemur pranced up and down the fence importantly and Piper shuffled back into her burrow. Zoe's heart sank. She'd hoped that the puffling would enjoy a visit from Zoe's friends, but she seemed even sadder!

Soon it was time for the class to go home.

"All of your parents will be picking you up at the zoo gates so we'd better not keep them waiting," Miss Hawkins said. "And tomorrow morning I want everyone to write a poem about our visit to the zoo and the fascinating animals we've seen. Thank you so much, Zoe and Mrs Parker!"

As the class called goodbye and made their way back through the zoo, Meep leapt on to Zoe's shoulder. "That was great, wasn't it?" he chirped happily. "I really saved the day, didn't I, when Piper was being boring?"

"Meep!" hissed Zoe. "Piper isn't boring. She's just not very happy. And you didn't help by showing off."

Meep stared at Zoe. Then he jumped from her shoulder and scampered away. For a moment, Zoe thought about running after him, but then she decided against it. *Meep has to learn not to show off so much,* she thought.

"Do you want to try and feed Piper while I go and check in at the hospital?" Lucy asked. "She might want to eat now that there aren't so many people around."

"Of course," Zoe replied. She took the bucket of herring from her mum and went over to Piper's burrow.

"Hey, Piper, are you hungry?" she called.

Piper poked her head out of the burrow

and looked at Zoe.

"It's OK, everyone else has gone," Zoe reassured her.

The little puffling shuffled out and gave her wings a quick flap.

"Would you like some herring?" Zoe asked.

Piper put her head to one side as if she wasn't sure.

"What is it, Piper? What's wrong?"

Piper opened her brightly coloured beak and started to cheep.

"It's not like the fish you ate back at home?" Zoe said.

Piper shook her head. The poor little puffling looked so sad.

"I bet you must really be missing your home," Zoe said.

Piper gave a squawk and nodded.

"Sometimes it's nice to try new things though," Zoe said. "Just because it's different it doesn't mean you won't like it." She held a herring close to Piper's beak. "Go on, why don't you give it a try?"

Piper tilted her head to one side but just as Zoe thought she was about to say no again, Piper opened her beak wide and gobbled up the herring whole.

"Well?" Zoe said with a smile. "What do you think?"

Piper chirped happily and Zoe grinned. "I told you! Would you like another one?"

Piper nodded and flapped her wings.

When Zoe got back to the cottage that evening, Meep wasn't in his usual spot, waiting for her by the front door. "Where's Meep?" she asked Lucy, who was cooking dinner in the kitchen.

"I'm not sure. I haven't seen him since this afternoon," Lucy replied.

Zoe looked all around the house for the little lemur, checking his favourite places, like the bowl of bananas on the windowsill and the cosy armchair in the living room, where Meep liked to curl up and snooze. Finally she tried her bedroom.

As she pushed open the door, she spotted Meep on top of her wardrobe. He was huddled up in a furry ball, his arms crossed sulkily.

"Meep, what are you doing up there?" said Zoe gently. "Why don't you come down?"

Meep ignored her. "Meep, it's almost dinnertime," Zoe reminded him. Meep loved eating more than anything! "There are some lovely ripe bananas downstairs, and some fresh blueberries, and a big packet of your favourite sunflower seeds."

Zoe saw Meep hesitate for a moment, but then the little lemur shook his head firmly. "I don't like any of those things," he squeaked, turning away from her. "I'm picky picky picky. Just like Piper the puffin!"

When Zoe went to bed that night, Meep was still on top of the wardrobe. Zoe couldn't remember a night when Meep hadn't gone to sleep cuddled up by her feet. She slipped under the covers and switched off the light. Without Meep's small, warm, furry body at the foot of the bed, it felt very empty and lonely.

Wait a minute, she thought suddenly. *I'm feeling sad because I'm missing Meep – my*

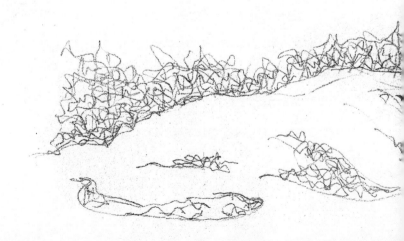

*best friend. Could that be the reason Piper is
so sad? What if she's missing her puffin friends
as well as her home?* Zoe thought of Piper's
enclosure. It was so lovely and peaceful
with its cosy burrow and pretty trees –
but it was missing one important thing.
Friends!

That's it! Zoe thought. *I need to find Piper
some friends – and fast!*

Chapter Five
Exciting News

When her mum called her for breakfast
the next morning, Zoe checked the end of
her bed for Meep. She'd been hoping he'd
come down in the night but he was still
on top of the wardrobe.

"It's breakfast time, Meep," she called
up to him. "Are you coming down?"

The little lemur crossed his arms and

shook his head.

"But you love breakfast!" Zoe exclaimed. "Don't you want to have some fruit? How about some tasty raisins?"

But Meep refused to move.

Zoe sighed. Maybe if she went downstairs Meep would get hungry and come and join her. And she needed to go and see her mum; she wanted to tell her about the idea she'd had just before falling asleep last night. Zoe hurried downstairs and burst into the kitchen.

"Goodness, Zoe, you're very excited about breakfast!" Lucy joked as she poured her a bowl of cereal and put it on the kitchen table.

"Mum, I've had an idea!" Zoe said breathlessly. "I think Piper is unhappy because she's lonely. We need to find her some friends."

Lucy nodded thoughtfully. "You could be right, Zoe. Puffins are very sociable birds, after all – they like living in groups. But there are no other puffins at the Rescue Zoo for Piper to live with. She's the only one."

"Who's the only one?" a voice boomed, and Great-Uncle Horace walked in. He was wearing his long coat and scarf, and Kiki was perched on his shoulder.

"Great-Uncle Horace!" Zoe exclaimed. "We were just talking about Piper. I think she's feeling really lonely being the only puffin at the zoo."

"Is that so?" Great-Uncle Horace sat down and Kiki hopped on to the table. "Well now, this is very interesting indeed."

Zoe waited for him to say something

else but Great-Uncle Horace kept quiet,
his bright eyes twinkling.

"Maybe we should ask Will to put her in with some of the other sea birds," Lucy suggested.

"Maybe. . ." Great-Uncle Horace said. "Or maybe we could turn some unhappy news into a happy ending."

Zoe stared at him. "What do you mean?"

"Kiki, we have work to do!" Great-Uncle Horace snapped his fingers and Kiki hopped back on to his shoulder. "We were about to go on a mission to Outer Mongolia to study the eating habits of the long-horned antelope but first we have something to organise." Great-Uncle Horace got to his feet and rushed out of the room.

"What was that about?" Zoe asked, puzzled.

"I have no idea!" Lucy replied.

"So shall I go and ask Will if we could try introducing Piper to the penguins?" Zoe asked.

Lucy nodded.

When Zoe got to the penguin enclosure she found Will feeding the birds their breakfast from a big bucket of fish.

"I think that's a great idea," Will said when Zoe told him her plan.

"So do I!" Pip chirped, flapping his wings excitedly. "I can't wait to meet a puffin. I'd love to be her friend."

Zoe hurried round to Piper's enclosure. The little puffling was standing by the side of the stream, looking down into the water.

"Piper, I've got some great news!" she

said. "I've found you a new friend."

Piper tilted her head to one side and cheeped.

"No, he isn't a puffin," Zoe replied. "He's a penguin but I'm sure you'll really like him. Come on, I'll take you to see him now."

She crouched down beside Piper and very gently cupped the little bird in her hands.

But as Zoe carried Piper into the penguin enclosure, the little puffling began chirping nervously, and shuffled into a corner as soon as Zoe put her down. The other birds cheeped a friendly greeting, and Pip even brought a fish over for Piper – but Zoe could see that the tiny puffin still wasn't happy.

"What's wrong?" Zoe whispered, stroking Piper's silky feathers.

Piper hung her head and gave a sad little cheep.

"You're missing your puffin friends?" Zoe said.

Piper nodded.

"Oh, Piper, I'm sorry." Zoe picked up the puffling and gave her a gentle hug.

Once Zoe had returned Piper to her enclosure she made her way back through the zoo. There must be something she could do to make Piper feel happier. There must be some way of helping her make new friends. Then she saw Great-Uncle Horace striding towards her, Kiki flying in circles above his head.

"Zoe, I have news!" he called.

Zoe ran to meet him. "What is it, Great-Uncle Horace?"

"There have been some terrible storms at sea recently, which have led to a lot of puffins being washed up on the coast. Obviously that's very sad news," he added. "But the better news is that a lot of puffins have been taken to a sea-life rescue centre just a few miles from here. Too many puffins, in fact."

"What do you mean, too many?" Zoe asked.

"Well, the sea-life centre is struggling to cope. So I just phoned them and told them that we would be happy to help, seeing as they have too many puffins and we don't have enough."

"Does that mean. . ." Zoe looked at him excitedly.

"We're taking some of the puffins off their hands," Great-Uncle Horace announced. "They're arriving tomorrow and then Piper shall have all the friends she needs."

"Great-Uncle Horace, that is excellent news!" Zoe exclaimed, giving him a hug.

Just then, she spotted a group of children walking through the zoo wearing party hats and carrying balloons. A brilliant idea popped into her head. "We could have a party!" she said, and her eyes opened wide. "A puffin party for Piper and her new friends when they arrive. It could be a surprise. We could invite all the zoo keepers and Great-Uncle Horace, and we could even ask my teacher and the children from my class."

And, she thought to herself, *a party might cheer up Meep too.*

When she got back home Zoe ran straight up to her bedroom. "Meep, you have to come down!" she called to the top of her wardrobe.

A pair of ears appeared over the edge of the wardrobe door, followed by two large golden eyes and a little nose. "What do you want?" Meep sniffed.

"I need your help. We're going to throw a party for Piper. A surprise puffin party!" explained Zoe. "We'll have balloons and games and all your favourite party food. And we can play party games too. What games would you

98

like to play, Meep?"

"How about 'hide the puffin'?" Meep
said grumpily.

Zoe put her hands on her hips and
looked at Meep very seriously. "Meep,
I just don't understand why you're
behaving like this," she said. "Poor Piper
hasn't done anything wrong. It's not her
fault that she's feeling sad and lonely, is
it?"

Meep scowled. "I don't know why she's
feeling sad and lonely when she's stolen
my best friend!" he answered crossly.
"I'm the one who should be feeling sad,
not her!"

Zoe stared at the little lemur. "Meep,
what are you talking about?"

"I know you like Piper best now,"
muttered Meep. "You picked her to do

your project on, instead of me. You invited all your schoolfriends to come to the zoo to see her, instead of me."

"Oh, Meep," Zoe said. "You don't think I like Piper better than you, do you?"

Meep nodded miserably.

Zoe couldn't help laughing. So this was why Meep had been acting so strangely recently. He wasn't being mean, he was worried Zoe didn't love him any more. "Meep, you've got this all wrong! You're my best friend – and you always will be. I just wanted to help Piper settle in and find some friends of her own. And I'd like us to be her friends, Meep. But you're still my favourite friend of all."

"Really? Do you promise?" Meep chirped, peering down from the wardrobe.

"I promise!" said Zoe, grinning as the

little lemur jumped down and into her
arms for a big cuddle.

Chapter Six
Puffin Party!

"It's puffin party time!" said Zoe excitedly.

It was Saturday and Zoe had just made the final touches to the decorations. Bright-orange balloons to match Piper's feet were strung up at the entrance to the enclosure, bobbing gently in the breeze. A colourful, stripy tablecloth to match

Piper's beak had been spread over a table just outside the enclosure. It was covered with party food. There were sandwiches, sausage rolls, cakes, biscuits, and a big bowl of fruit for Meep. Next to the table was a bucket filled with shiny silver herring, an orange ribbon tied to the handle.

All the guests were waiting by the gate to the enclosure. Zoe saw her teacher and some of her schoolfriends, as well as lots of the zoo keepers. Great-Uncle Horace was welcoming everyone, while Lucy was handing out drinks. Even Mr Pinch had turned up, though he was looking at the table of food very suspiciously. "Sandwiches! I hate sandwiches," he muttered. "They make so many crumbs!"

In fact, the only guest who wasn't there

yet was Piper! The little puffling was
tucked up inside her burrow, fast asleep.
Zoe couldn't wait to wake her up and
tell her that there was a surprise party,
just for her.

"If it's puffin party time, does that mean
I can start eating now?" asked Meep,
eyeing the bowl of fruit hopefully. "I'm

starving!" Because Meep had spent so long pretending to be picky, he had even more of an appetite than before.

Zoe giggled. "Just a few berries then," she said. "But I need you to do something for me."

"What's that?" asked Meep, stuffing a handful of juicy blueberries in his mouth and reaching for another.

"I want you to make a really special effort to be Piper's friend and help her enjoy the party," she explained. "I think you'll be good at that, Meep. What do you think?"

Meep puffed up his chest proudly. "I can definitely do that, Zoe!"

"Zoe!" called Lucy. "I think it's time for the guests to come inside, don't you?"

Zoe nodded. "And when everyone's ready, we'll bring out Piper."

The line of guests streamed inside the enclosure, chatting quietly.

On her shoulder, Meep clapped his tiny paws together excitedly. "Let's go and get Piper."

Zoe and Meep made their way over to Piper's burrow. "Piper, it's us — Zoe and

Meep!" said Zoe, kneeling down and peering inside.

The little puffling was snuggled inside her cosy burrow, fast asleep. As Zoe gently whispered her name, she blinked her eyes open. When she saw Meep, she gave a nervous squeak.

"Piper, I'm sorry I was a bit grumpy before," chirped Meep. "Will you come out and play?"

Piper looked uncertain.

"Come on, Piper! I'm really good fun, I promise!" Meep hopped up and down on his hind paws, then turned a cartwheel. He crossed his eyes and stuck his tongue out cheekily. Zoe giggled at her little friend's antics, and even Piper squeaked with laughter. Very slowly, the little puffling shuffled out of her burrow.

She gave a curious cheep when she saw the party guests.

"Surprise!" Zoe said with a smile. "All these people are here to see you, Piper. It's a puffin party," she explained, smiling.

"There's always lots of tasty food at a party," added Meep. "That's the best thing about them, I think."

"I don't know," Zoe said with a grin. "I think the best thing about this party is the special guests."

Piper gave another curious cheep.

"You want to know who the special guests are?" Zoe replied. "I'll let Great-Uncle Horace introduce them."

Zoe and Meep led Piper over to Great-Uncle Horace. "Piper's ready to meet her special guests," she told him.

"Excellent!" Great-Uncle Horace

replied. Then he walked over to a crate at the side of the enclosure. "Out you come," he said, lifting the lid.

The crowd gasped as, one by one, five puffins hopped from the crate, flapping their wings.

Piper's beak fell open in surprise.

"They've come to live here," Zoe explained. "With you."

Piper began hopping up and down excitedly. When the other puffins saw her they came waddling over. They each took it in turns to nuzzle Piper with their beaks.

"Oh look, it's like they're cuddling!" Zoe exclaimed.

Piper chirped something to the other puffins and they followed her over to the burrows.

"Good job you dug so many, eh, Zoe?" Great-Uncle Horace chuckled.

As the other puffins inspected their burrows Piper let out a loud, joyful squeak.

Zoe giggled. "That's the noisiest we've ever heard you, Piper! Now, why don't you all come and join the party – and maybe try the party tea?"

Piper led the other puffins over to the party guests.

As everyone took pictures of the puffins, Piper gave a happy squeak. Finally Zoe carried her over to the party tea table.

"It's time to eat!" she said. "How about a lovely herring, Piper?"

She held up a fish, but Piper looked a little unsure.

"Go on, Piper," said Meep. "Eating is one of the best things in the whole world and it's really easy. Watch." He tossed a blackberry into his mouth, gobbled it down and rubbed his tummy happily. "Now it's your turn!"

Zoe beamed as the little puffin copied Meep, opening her beak and gobbling the herring down, and then patting her tummy with her wings! "Brilliant, Piper!" she whispered. "Would you like another?"

"Zoe, I think Piper might even have a bigger appetite than me!" chattered Meep as Piper gulped down

three more fish.

As the party guests all laughed and chatted, Zoe grinned. Everything had worked out. She and Meep were best friends again, Piper was happy at last and the Rescue Zoo had not one, but SIX new puffins!

If you enjoyed Piper's story,
look out for:

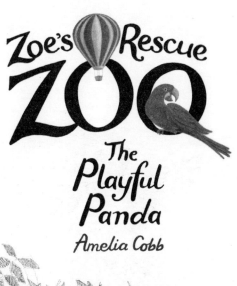

Zoe's Rescue
ZOO
The
Playful
Panda
Amelia Cobb

Chapter One

A Treat for Daisy

Zoe Parker grinned as she raced down the path. It was Saturday morning at the Rescue Zoo and Zoe was on her way to visit some of her favourite animals. Halfway down the path she stopped at a wooden gate and reached for the pretty silver paw-print charm on her necklace.

This was no ordinary necklace – it

opened the door to every single enclosure
in the Rescue Zoo! It had been a present
from her Great-Uncle Horace, who had
built the zoo, and Zoe never took it off.
She held the charm against a small panel
on the gate and with a quiet click it
swung open.

Zoe walked into a warm, wide plain,
covered in tall grass and lush trees. Just
beyond the gate was the house where
the giraffes slept, a tall red-brick building
with a high arched doorway. Zoe shaded
her eyes from the sunshine and saw the
herd gathered at the other end of the
enclosure, drinking from a sparkling
stream. By the gate stood a wheelbarrow
full of fresh straw, and a large garden fork.
The giraffe keeper, Frankie, had promised
Zoe she could help out this morning, and

everything she needed was ready for her!

Zoe grabbed the wheelbarrow and pushed it into the giraffe house. She picked up the fork and began lifting the straw out, spreading it carefully on the ground so that the giraffes would have clean, comfortable bedding that night.

She hummed happily as she worked, enjoying the warm breeze and wondering where her best friend had got to. He had dashed off along the path in front of her that morning, too excited to slow down!

Suddenly the straw in the wheelbarrow started to wriggle. Zoe watched curiously as it shook from side to side. Then a furry little head popped out and a pair of huge, golden eyes blinked cheekily at her.

"Meep!" laughed Zoe. "There you are, you naughty thing!"

With a cheerful chirp, the tiny creature sprang out of the wheelbarrow and climbed up on to Zoe's shoulder, sending bits of straw everywhere. Meep was a grey mouse lemur. He was very small with a long, curling tail and soft, delicate ears that stuck up in the air. He'd come to the zoo when he was just a baby, and lived with Zoe and her mum in their cottage.

"I wondered where you'd disappeared to, Meep. You're supposed to be helping me tidy the giraffe enclosure, not making a mess!" Zoe shook her head but couldn't help smiling. The little lemur was so cute that she could never *really* tell him off.

As she finished spreading out the straw, Zoe heard a gentle bray behind her and turned around. The youngest member of the giraffe herd, Daisy, had come over to greet them. She was just a few months old but she was still more than twice as tall as Zoe!

Zoe's Rescue Zoo

**Look out for MORE
amazing animal adventures
at the Rescue Zoo!**

The Secret Rescuers

**If you enjoyed this book,
we think you'll love The Secret Rescuers!**

The Rescue Princesses

Have you read the brilliant Rescue Princesses books? And look out for new Rescue Princesses, coming soon.